Bring on That Beat

Rachel Isadora

G. P. Putnam's Sons

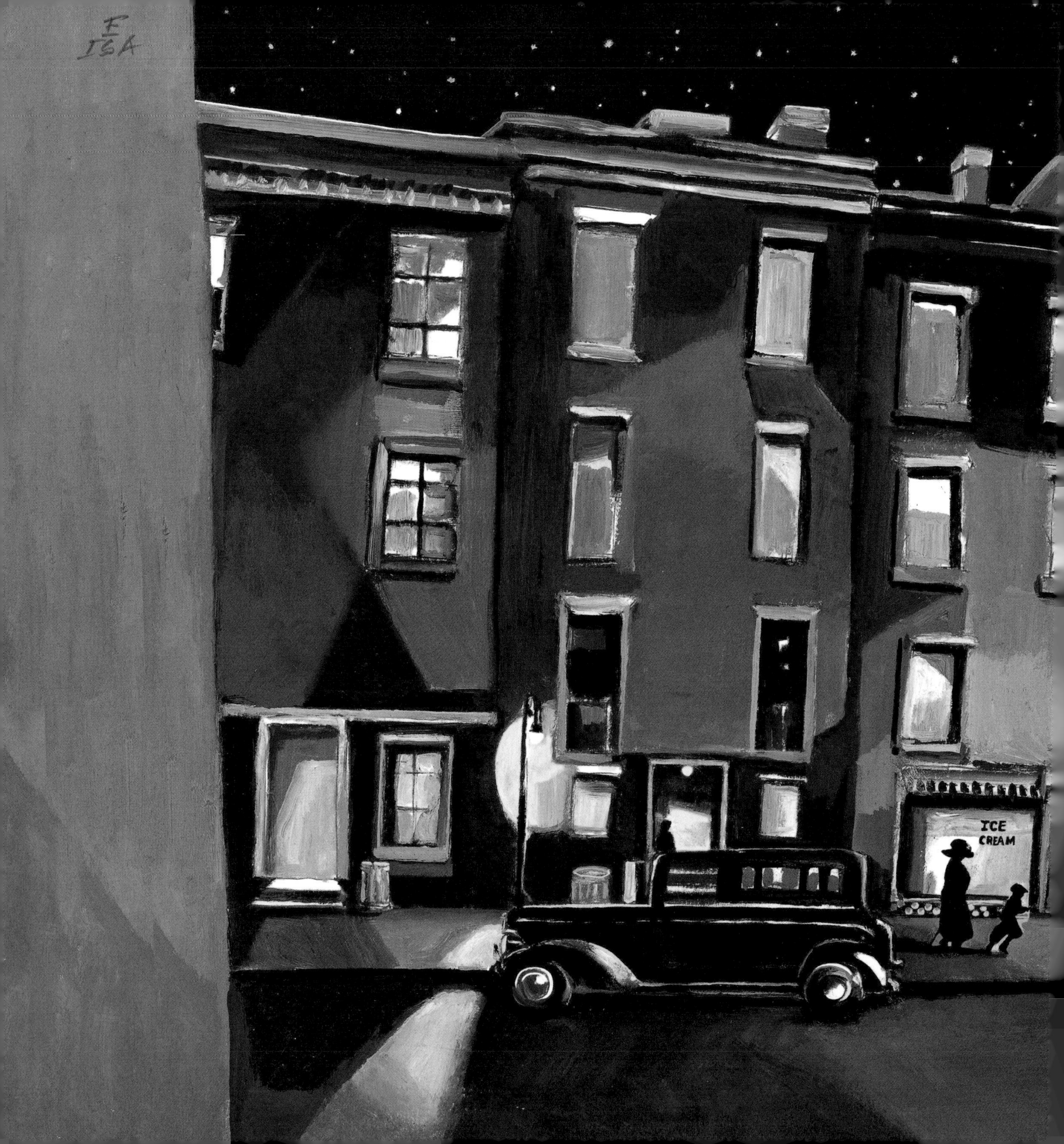
ICE
CREAM

Saxophone jive,
Keep us alive.

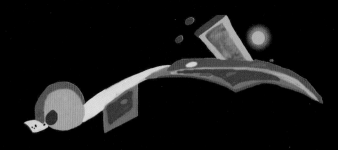

Trumpet a song,
Groove the night long.

Bring on that beat
Where we all meet.

Swing in the night,
Dance by the light.

Bring on that beat,
Watch her two feet.

Duke Ellington—
King o' the sun.
Cool as a cat,
He's where it's at.

Stars meet the blue,
Sway with us too.

All over town,
Hear that hot sound.

When you rap and you rhyme,
Remember that time—
When cats played the beat,
It was jazz on the street.

For Mady, who never misses a beat . . .

G. P. PUTNAM'S SONS,
a division of Penguin Putnam Books for Young Readers,
345 Hudson Street, New York, NY 10014.
G. P. Putnam's Sons, Reg. U.S. Pat. & Tm. Off.
Published simultaneously in Canada.
Printed in Hong Kong by South China Printing Co. (1988) Ltd.
Designed by Sharon Murray Jacobs.
Text set in twenty-two point Stone Sans Bold.
Rachel began this book with a great love of jazz. She painted the black-and-white pictures in oil.
These were overlaid with watercolored designs on the computer.
Library of Congress Cataloging-in-Publication Data
Isadora, Rachel. Bring on that beat / by Rachel Isadora.
p. cm. Summary: Illustrations and rhyming text evoke the rhythms of jazz music.
[1. Jazz—Fiction. 2. Afro-Americans—Fiction. 3. Stories in rhyme.] I. Title.
PZ8.3.I76 Br 2002 [E]—dc21 99-054837
ISBN 0-399-23232-X
1 3 5 7 9 10 8 6 4 2
FIRST IMPRESSION